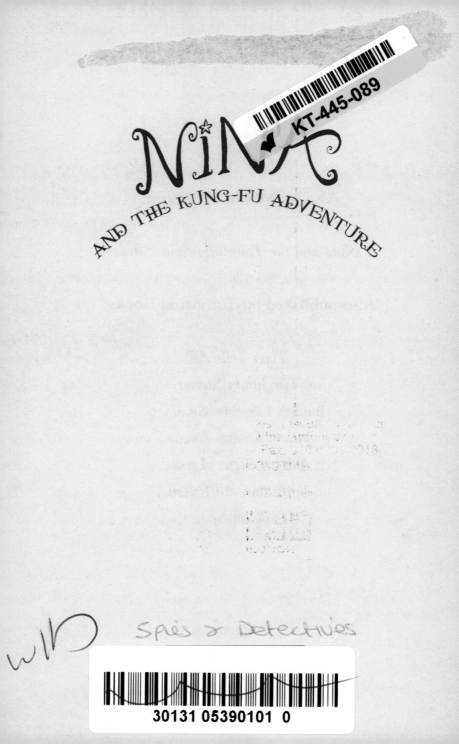

NINA

AND THE KUNG-FU ADVENTURE

Also by Madhvi Ramani:

Nina and the Travelling Spice Shed

Also published by Tamarind Books:

Tiger Tells All
The Julian Stories
Julian's Glorious Summer
Julian, Dream Doctor
Julian, Secret Agent
Spike and Ali Enson
Spike in Space

NINA

AND THE KUNG-FU ADVENTURE

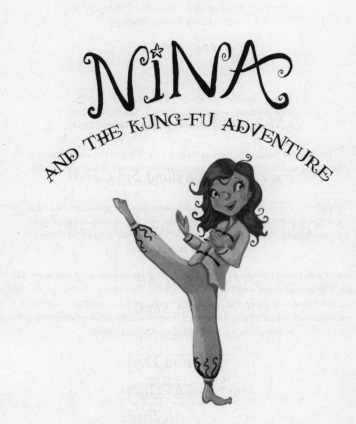

Madhvi Ramani

Illustrated by Erica-Jane Waters

Tamarind

NINA AND THE KUNG-FU ADVENTURE
A TAMARIND BOOK 978 1 848 53091 1

First Published in Great Britain by Tamarind Books,
an imprint of Random House Children's Publishers UK
A Random House Group Company

This edition published 2013

1 3 5 7 9 10 8 6 4 2

The Random House Group Limited supports the Forest Stewardship Council® (FSC®),
the leading international forest-certification organisation. Our books carrying the FSC label are
printed on FSC®-certified paper. FSC is the only forest-certification scheme supported by the
leading environmental organisations, including Greenpeace. Our paper procurement policy can
be found at www.randomhouse.co.uk/environment.

Set in Bembo MT

Tamarind Books are published by Random House Children's Publishers UK,
61–63 Uxbridge Road, London W5 5SA

www.**tamarindbooks**.co.uk
www.**randomhousechildrens**.co.uk
www.**randomhouse**.co.uk

Addresses for companies within The Random House Group Limited
can be found at: www.randomhouse.co.uk/offices.htm

THE RANDOM HOUSE GROUP Limited Reg. No. 954009

A CIP catalogue record for this book is available from the British Library.

Printed and bound by Clays Ltd, St Ives plc

For Herr Doctor Keisinger,
a genius no less

Chapter One

Without wings often I fly,
Seasons change as I pass by.
Can't turn me back, try as you may
Watch me lest I run away.

"Can anyone tell me the answer to this riddle?" asked Miss Matthews, pointing at the board.

Nina screwed up her face in concentration. Something that flies and can't be turned back . . . It was . . . It was . . .

"Time," came a voice from behind her.

Nina frowned. She didn't need to look round to see who got the answer first; it was Lee Chen, the new boy from China. Nina wished that she was as clever as Lee.

The bell rang, and she was glad it was finally home time. She was staying over at Aunt Nishi's for the weekend. Nina loved it at her aunt's house. It was filled with old books and ancient artefacts, along with modern gadgets. She even had the latest computer games, and she taught Nina the cheats. Words such as "bedtime" or "homework" were never uttered in her house.

Aunt Nishi was some sort of computer whizz who worked for the government – although no one knew exactly what she did. Nina, however, suspected that there was a lot more to her aunt than her passion for cooking. She had seen Aunt Nishi shuffle documents stamped with the words TOP SECRET. She had even been let into a top secret herself: the shed in Aunt Nishi's garden was a teleportation machine. It could take you anywhere in the world in an instant! Although Aunt Nishi hadn't let her use it since her last adventure in India, Nina was hoping that she would eventually relent. The very thought of that musty old shed, filled with jars of spices, almost made her burst with excitement. But she couldn't tell anyone – that was the thing about secrets. As she walked out of the classroom and across the playground, she thought about where she might go next . . . Hawaii, New Zealand, maybe even the North Pole.

Her daydream was interrupted by a wailing sound – it was Lee. Simon, the biggest bully in school, had lifted him up and was about to throw him into one of the huge bins at the end of the playground.

"Leave him alone!" called Nina, stomping over to them.

"Keep your big nose out of this, else I'll put you in there too," growled Simon.

Nina looked at the stinky bin. It was filled with rotten leftovers. She certainly didn't want to end up in there. Then again, she couldn't just stand by and watch Lee get thrown in. But what could she do? Suddenly she had an idea. She charged at Simon's legs, making him fall over and drop Lee.

"Run!" cried Nina, and they dashed out of the school gates. They were both small compared to Simon, but they managed to out-run him. Just before they lost him, however, they caught his last angry words behind them.

"Just wait till Monday! It's binning for both of you!"

Chapter Two

"Great," said Nina when they stopped to catch their breath. "Now look what you've done – we're in for it on Monday."

"Sorry. It seems like all I do is cause trouble everywhere I go. My aunt's going to kill me when she sees the state of my new school uniform," said Lee, looking at his scraped trousers and crumpled shirt.

Nina felt a little sorry for him. "I'm going to my aunt's after school too. She lives nearby – why don't you come and see if she can help fix it up?" she said.

★ ★ ★

Aunt Nishi was, in fact, very enthusiastic about helping Lee with his uniform.

"A perfect opportunity to test out my Whizzbanger!" she said as she threw Lee's uniform into a peculiar-looking machine and pressed the red button. Lee, now in his PE kit, looked at Nina worriedly as the room filled with whizzing and banging sounds.

"No need to look so apprehensive," said Aunt Nishi. "The Whizzbanger was invented by my good friend Herr Professor Doctor

Keisinger. A genius, no less. He didn't want to waste time worrying about things like clothes so he invented this; it washes, dries, irons and mends holes in your garments at high velocity. He's been wearing the same suit ever since he invented it in 1987."

As the machine whizzed faster, Aunt Nishi and Lee talked about velocity and physics and stuff that Nina didn't understand. Steam started to rise from the curved pipe sticking out of the top of the Whizzbanger, but they didn't seem to notice. Nina was glad when their conversation was interrupted by three loud bangs, and Lee's uniform popped out of the machine, sparkling crisp.

"Wow! Thanks!"

"I wish my aunt was cool like yours," said Lee as they made their way to the living room to play computer games while Aunt Nishi prepared dinner. "She's always going on about her peace and quiet. She never had children, so she's not used to having me around. Then again, if it weren't for her, I'd be stuck in an orphanage in Beijing right now."

"Oh. What happened to your parents?"

Nina was shocked when she heard Lee's story. He had lived a normal, happy life in Beijing until about a month ago. Then, one day, he came home from school to find that his family's apartment had been turned upside down and his parents had disappeared. The police suspected that they had been kidnapped. However, they could find no reason why anyone would want to kidnap his father, an English Literature professor, and his mother, a kung-fu expert. They soon ran out of leads and dropped the case.

"I think I found a clue though," said Lee.

"What is it?"

"There's no point. I can't figure out what it means."

"Well, maybe I can," said Nina.

Lee looked at her doubtfully, then tore a blank page out of his workbook and started scribbling something down. He paused, scratched his head, then continued to write.

"It's a riddle – a bit like the ones we did in English today," he said, crossing out some words and replacing them with new ones. "The old, yellowing paper it was printed on was hanging in a frame in our hallway for as long as I can remember. Anyway, this riddle was the only thing missing from our ransacked apartment. I told the police, but they aren't interested in mysteries from the past, just cold, hard facts," he said, tapping his pencil against his forehead.

Nina watched Lee struggle to finish writing out the riddle. Maybe he wasn't so smart after all.

"Here you go," he said, handing her the paper. "The original was in Chinese, so I had to translate."

Oh. That explains it, thought Nina. She looked at the paper. It read:

Red and gold we are for luck
Take us from the place of duck
Trail the brown then yellow snake
Till the place warriors bake
There you'll see our special key
That can set these forces free.

Nina was baffled. Maybe Lee was right to assume that she wouldn't be able to solve it. She suggested that they put their heads together for the rest of the evening to try to crack it.

They phoned Lee's aunt, who was happy to let him stay over at Aunt Nishi's because it meant she could have some peace and quiet. Lee's aunt didn't sound so bad – at least she let him do what he wanted. Nina would never be allowed to stay over at someone else's house so easily.

Aunt Nishi was also pleased that Nina had company. It meant that she could test out one of her new fusion food recipes on her guests, then get round to throwing all her old saris into the Whizzbanger.

Although dinner was tasty, Nina didn't eat much of her egg-noodle vindaloo. She was keen to get back to the riddle.

Lee was sure that the first line referred to his parents, because everyone called them the lucky couple – although he didn't know why. The second line, which mentioned the place of duck, was more difficult. They looked at a map of China in one of Aunt Nishi's big old atlases and surfed the internet looking for anywhere that had a duck-related name, famous duck statues and even vast duck populations. However, by 11 o'clock they were ready to give up.

"Doesn't matter," said Lee. "It was silly to think we could solve it. Even if we did find out what it meant, we wouldn't be able to do much. We're just kids."

But exhausted as she was, Nina couldn't get to sleep. She kept thinking about how terribly Lee must miss his parents and his life in Beijing. If only she were cleverer, then she would be able to help.

From what she had found out, Beijing seemed like an exciting place. She added it to her mental list of places she would like to visit. After all, she did love Chinese food. Her favourite was Peking duck.

Nina sat up in bed – it was as if a bolt of lightning had struck her. She got up, changed, and crept out into the hallway. Aunt Nishi's soft snores trembled through the air.

Nina peeked into her bedroom. Her aunt lay on her back, silver curls spread out around her head. On the bedside table, the tiny key to the spice shed glinted in the moonlight.

Nina knew it was wrong to take things without permission, but this was important. Her heart thudded as she picked up the key, which was attached to a thin gold chain. She hung it around her neck and backed out into the hallway again. She tiptoed into Lee's room and shook him.

"Oh no – is it time for school already?" he grumbled, still half asleep.

"No, silly," said Nina. "I've solved the second line of the riddle!"

Chapter Three

"Arrgh! Something's scratching my legs!" groaned Lee. He was still wearing the PE kit he had gone to bed in.

"Shhh," said Nina. "Stop being a baby and hurry up – we're almost there."

"I don't think we should be doing this. I mean, we might get eaten by dangerous animals."

"Don't be ridiculous, we're only in Aunt Nishi's back garden," said Nina.

"Well, it's practically a jungle here. Hasn't your aunt heard of a lawnmower?"

Nina couldn't argue with that. The garden

was so overgrown and wild that it was almost impossible to make out the ramshackle shed that Aunt Nishi stored her spices in. Luckily, Nina knew exactly where it was.

When they got there, she took out the tiny gold key and fumbled around to find the lock. It was difficult, with only the dim light of the moon to help her, but eventually it clicked open and they stepped inside. The single bulb that dangled from the ceiling flickered on and the heavy door shut behind them. Nina's nostrils tingled as she breathed in the air, which was heavy with dust and spices.

"You brought me all the way here in the middle of the night to show me your aunt's spice collection?" said Lee, looking at the shelves stacked with hundreds of glass jars filled with different-coloured spices.

"Not exactly," said Nina, going over to the back of the shed, where a heap of objects was piled up: skis, a sombrero, diving equipment . . . She grabbed the broomstick leaning against the wall and pulled it forward like a lever. There was a low whining sound and a wide, flat screen came sliding down into the shed. It showed a detailed map of the world, accompanied by the words:

TOUCH SCREEN TO GO TO DESTINATION

"See!" said Nina. "This isn't just any old shed. It's a teleportation machine! Touch a

18

TOUCH SCREEN TO GO TO DESTINATION

place on the screen and you're there in an instant."

"That fusion food must be interfering with your head," said Lee, looking at Nina as if she were barking mad.

Nina had expected that sort of reaction, which is why she hadn't told anyone about the shed. That, and the fact that Aunt Nishi had sworn her to secrecy.

"You'll see as soon as we get to Beijing," she said.

"Beijing?"

"Yes. I was thinking about my favourite food, Peking duck, and remembered that Peking is the old name for Beijing—"

Lee smacked his palm against his forehead. "So Beijing must be the place of duck! 'Red and gold we are for luck' – that refers to my parents. 'Take us from the place of duck' – yes, somebody took them from Beijing!"

"And I bet the rest of the riddle tells us where they've been taken to. Ready?" said Nina, prodding Beijing on the map.

"Whoaa!" cried Lee as the shed began to tremble.

Nina held onto a shelf, while Lee shuffled around trying to keep his balance, as if doing a little dance. Nina thought she could see thousands of little particles whizzing around in the dim light. Lee fell backwards and landed on his bottom. Then everything was still.

The message on the screen now read:

WELCOME TO BEIJING, CHINA

Nina released her grip on the shelf and went to the door. Slowly, she pushed it open. Anything could be on the other side. She had learned her lesson last time, when she had stepped out of the shed in the middle of a Mumbai street and had almost been run over. She turned to Lee, who was dazzled by the daylight streaming in through the door.

"Come on," she said.

Chapter Four

"Why is it morning? Am I dreaming? Did I bump my head?" asked Lee as he followed Nina outside.

"No silly, we're in . . ." Nina looked around. The shed was in the middle of a huge, immaculately kept lawn. There wasn't a car, person, or shop in sight — not exactly what Nina expected a capital city to be like.

"The Bird's Nest!" cried Lee.

Nina looked at him quizzically.

"That's what we call the Olympic Stadium," he explained.

Of course. Nina had seen the Beijing

Olympics on television and recognized the
metal structure that curved around the
perimeter. The crisscrossing beams looked
like twigs placed one on top of another. While
Nina took in her surroundings, Lee chirped
on like an excited sparrow.

"So we're really here! No wonder it's light.
It's morning here! Wow!"

"The next line of the riddle says something
about trailing brown and yellow snakes,"

Nina said. "Let's investigate – we're on the path to finding your parents!"

The streets of Beijing were crowded and stuffy. Nina was baffled by the banners decorated with Chinese writing that ran down the sides of shops. Lee explained that Chinese was read from top to bottom, and had many more characters than English.

Along with the shops she didn't recognize were familiar brands like Nike and Adidas and restaurants like McDonald's and Kentucky Fried Chicken, but Nina wasn't interested in all that fast food – she was interested in the even faster food being cooked along the sides of the streets.

Lee noticed this. "No soggy cornflakes for breakfast here! Come on, let's have some baozi – my favourite!" he said, stopping in front of a stall piled with steaming white buns. Lee ordered, then turned to Nina.

"Erm, you don't happen to have any Yuan, do you? I had some Chinese money, but it's at my aunt's place."

Nina shook her head. The vendor pointed at the gold chain around her neck, and she understood what he meant. She wanted to try the buns, but if she swapped the necklace for them, where would she keep the key to the spice shed? The pockets of her trousers were too deep, and she was afraid it would get lost.

Lee's T-shirt, however, had a little pocket with a button, so she detached the key and gave it to him for safekeeping. Then she exchanged the necklace for the buns.

Nina frowned as she watched Lee grab a baozi with his chopsticks, lift it to his mouth and take a bite. She had never been able to use chopsticks. She tried to copy him, but just as she was about to put the bun in her mouth, it slipped back onto the plate.

When Lee saw this, he gasped. "You shouldn't lick your chopsticks," he said. "It's rude!"

Nina felt annoyed at herself for not being able to do such a simple thing. At this rate she would never get to taste the baozi. Just then, Lee picked up a leaflet. While he was busy reading it, Nina shoved the chopsticks into her pocket and picked up the bun with her fingers. It was soft and warm and filled with brown sugar. Once she finished eating, she looked over Lee's shoulder.

"It's an advert for a kung-fu school," he explained, "and I recognize the name of the teacher: Master Zhong. He's one of the best in China, and he used to teach my mother! Kung-fu teachers are the keepers of ancient knowledge. Come on – he's bound to know what the riddle means!"

They followed the map on the leaflet, and soon found their way to the kung-fu school. Through the gold lattice gates, they saw a courtyard filled with rows of children standing to attention. At the front was a short bald man with bushy eyebrows and a long white beard, wearing a black cloak. Nina studied the wise lines across his forehead and around his eyes, and guessed that he was Master Zhong.

Suddenly, Master Zhong looked at Nina and Lee, and said something in a stern voice that Nina didn't understand, but made her heart jump with fear.

Chapter Five

"Master Zhong thinks we're late for his lesson," said Lee, pulling the gate open. "We'd better join in. I don't think he's the kind of person we should get on the wrong side of."

The next hour was excruciating. They did press-ups, sit-ups, high jumps, star jumps, squats — and that was just the warm-up. Then they practised spinning kicks and flying kicks before going on to play-fight each other. Nina enjoyed watching the other children sparring; they were so graceful, it looked like they were dancing rather than fighting. Even better was watching the advanced students, who could break a plank of wood in two with one kick. Nina tried to copy them, but just ended up hurting her foot. Master Zhong kept going on about "key energy" while she was doing this, but she had no idea what he meant.

After that, they did a "key building exercise". Master Zhong told them to sit down, breathe deeply and imagine they were moving their hands around a ball of energy, floating just above their laps. Nina thought this was the silliest thing she'd ever been asked to do, but after a while she began to feel a growing heat between her palms. Then Master Zhong called the end of the lesson and the sensation faded.

Nina and Lee flopped down onto the floor, while the other children cleared out of the courtyard. A shadow fell over them. It was Master Zhong.

Lee jumped up and introduced himself as the son of Kiki Lhang, who was once his student. When Lee mentioned his mother's name, Master Zhong's black eyes flickered, then a broad smile cracked over his face.

"Well, why didn't you say so? I haven't seen Kiki for years, but I couldn't forget her. She was my best student!" he said. After a pause, he added, "Although you certainly didn't inherit her talent."

"But you . . ." he said, turning to Nina. "You have good key."

Nina smiled, pleased that she was better

than Lee at something. Then she asked, "What's 'key'?"

"Come, let me invite you to lunch," laughed Master Zhong, "I'll explain."

At the noodle place opposite the kung-fu school, Master Zhong explained that "qi energy" was an inner power that, if you concentrated, you could use to do amazing things.

"In that last exercise, did you feel something between your hands?"

Nina nodded.

"That was your qi energy. If you practise, you can use it to kick harder, move faster, think clearer. You can even make a pair of chopsticks fly through the air like daggers!"

Fat chance, thought Nina. She was having a hard enough time just trying to use her chopsticks to eat the vegetable chow mein in front of her. She was starting to get the hang of it, but kept dropping one chopstick on the floor.

Luckily for Nina, Master Zhong and Lee became engrossed in a conversation about the riddle and the disappearance of his parents. This meant she could shove the dirty chopstick into her pocket and grab a new one from the box in the middle of the table without anyone noticing.

However, when she did this for the third time, Master Zhong shot her a chilling look. "If you drop a chopstick, you must abandon both of them and take an entirely new pair. You should never separate chopsticks, for they belong together – like yin and yang."

He turned to Lee. "It's a bit like your parents. They belong together like yin and yang. Your mother is yang because she is fiery and strong like the colour red, and your father is yin, calm and knowledgeable like gold. Together, they are the perfect combination and have the highest qi energy. That's why they are the lucky couple."

"So, what does the rest of the riddle mean?" asked Lee. He and Nina looked at Master Zhong expectantly.

Master Zhong's black eyes flickered. "I'm sorry, but I have no idea."

Chapter Six

Nina and Lee wandered around Beijing feeling lost and forlorn as they tried to work out what the "brown then yellow snake" meant. Master Zhong had been their best bet, and they dreaded having to return to England in the spice shed without discovering what had happened to Lee's parents.

When Lee pointed out a famous snake restaurant, Nina became excited.

"Maybe that has something to do with it! After all, the 'place of duck' had something to do with food, and now here's a— What *is* a snake restaurant, anyway?"

Lee looked at Nina as if to say, *Isn't it obvious?*

"A restaurant where— No!" said Nina. Her skin crawled at the idea of eating snakes.

"It's an old tradition. Snake is very good for you actually."

"What does it taste like?"

Lee scratched his head, and then said, "Like chicken."

"Let's see if the menu has any clues," said Nina.

"OK," said Lee, and began to read it out loud:

MENU
SNAKE
Restaurant

SNAKE SOUP
❧
CANTONESE-STYLE
Fricasséed Snake
❧
BRAISED COBRA WITH CITRONELLA
❧
SAUTÉED WATER SNAKE WITH
SOY SAUCE AND GINGER
❧
LEOPARD SNAKE HOT POT

Nina and Lee looked at each other and shrugged. They moved on.

As Nina walked around the city, she thought about opposites – yin and yang. Beijing was made up of very old parts, which were like yin to its very modern parts, yang. Nina's favourite part was the Forbidden City, which was very old. It was rich with red lanterns,

green dragons and gold statues of strange beasts. In the Hall of Supreme Harmony, she gaped at the most ornate throne she had ever seen. Once, Chinese emperors had sat on it. Now it was a tourist attraction, because China was no longer ruled by an emperor. The wall that surrounded the Forbidden City was around 500 years old, which Nina thought was quite impressive.

"That's nothing. You should see the Great Wall of China. It's older and it can even be seen from space!" said Lee.

"Really?" said Nina.

"Sure," said Lee. "It's because it's so long. It snakes through the whole of China." He paused. "Wait a minute. The wall was made of soil, wood and bricks, so it's brownish in colour. The wall is the brown snake!"

To celebrate their success, they treated themselves to special fried rice, using the money that Master Zhong had kindly given them.

It was easier to eat rice with chopsticks.

Nina just had to hold them together and shovel the rice into her mouth. However, she was much slower than Lee, who had already finished his meal by the time she was halfway through.

Nina looked up, and noticed Lee staring at her fish-eyed.

"Oh no, what have I done wrong with the chopsticks now?" she said, sticking them in her rice and folding her arms.

"I've figured out what the yellow snake is! It's the Yellow River! It also snakes through China, and even crosses paths with the wall!" he said. Suddenly a look of horror came over his face.

"Your chopsticks are standing straight up in your rice," he said. "That's a bad sign. It means death."

Lee stood up. "There's no time to lose. I'm going to see Master Zhong. He might be able to figure out the rest of the riddle now that we've solved the third line. I'll meet you there."

Nina looked at the ceramic chopsticks sticking out of her bowl of rice. An uneasy feeling came over her as she watched Lee go.

Chapter Seven

By the time Nina got to the kung-fu school, the sun was low in the sky. Master Zhong was locking the door to his building. Nina pulled the gate open and walked across the empty courtyard to meet him. She guessed that lessons were over for the day.

"Where's Lee?" asked Nina.

"I thought he was with you."

"No – he said he was coming here. He solved the third line: the brown snake is the Great Wall of China, and the yellow snake is the Yellow River. He's so clever. I would never have been able to get that. Anyway, he was going to ask for your help with the rest of the riddle."

"Oh dear, I haven't seen him. And now I must be on my way. I have a pressing engagement," said Master Zhong. A black van waited outside the gates. The characters of his kung-fu school were printed in red along its side.

"But Master Zhong, all this has something to do with the riddle. I know it. We have to do something!" said Nina. A picture of the chopsticks standing up in the rice flashed through her mind.

"I really don't see what we can do. As you

said, Lee is very clever. That's how he got so far in solving the riddle. Even I can't figure it out. And you just said you wouldn't be able to either," said Master Zhong, hurrying towards the gates.

Nina grabbed his sleeve. "But I got the place of duck!"

Master Zhong stopped and looked into her eyes. "Well, let me tell you something, Nina. The riddle gets harder as it goes along. You'd have to be a genius to work it out."

Nina's heart sank.

"Look, I'll get in touch with the police and have some people look out for Lee. You just run along home," he said, and then paused. He must have sensed her disappointment because his eyes softened and he hurried back into the building to fetch something. He returned with a narrow object, wrapped in red silk.

"For you. Just because you can't solve the riddle doesn't mean you don't have other good qualities," he said.

Nina took the object and unfolded the cloth. Inside lay a pair of solid gold chopsticks.

"In Chinese culture, chopsticks represent straightforwardness and honesty. Both are admirable qualities that I see you have."

Nina's heart lifted. Then she remembered how she had taken the key to the spice shed from Aunt Nishi's room. That hadn't been very straightforward or honest. Nina gasped. The key to the spice shed! Lee had it!

She looked up, but Master Zhong had already disappeared. She just managed to glimpse the back of his van, speeding away.

Chapter Eight

Nina sat on the steps of Master Zhong's kung-fu school. She was hoping that any minute now, Master Zhong or Lee would come through the gates, but the courtyard remained empty.

She tried to gather up her inner energy in order to think about the situation calmly, but she could not focus. She got up and paced the courtyard. In the corner of her eye, something flashed. She stopped pacing and walked over to where something glinted on the ground in the last rays of the sun. It was the key to the spice shed!

Lee *had* been here! And he had left Nina a clue! She picked up the key and closed her fist around it. Master Zhong had lied. She had no idea what he was up to, but she was determined to find out.

The way back to the spice shed was longer than she remembered, but she did not stop until she got there. When the door to the spice shed closed behind her, she sighed with relief. She was glad to be back here, away from the noise and bustle of the city. She put the key inside her shoe, where it would be safe.

Then she looked at the crumpled piece of paper on which the riddle was written. She breathed deeply and tried to focus her qi energy on deciphering the words in front of her:

Trail the brown then yellow snake
Till the place warriors bake.

She stared at the words until all other thoughts slipped away. Her forehead became hot. An image of warriors in full armour, dusted with flour and making cakes, popped into her mind. No, that wasn't right.

She regained her focus, and looked at the map of China on the screen. She traced the path of the Great Wall – the brown snake – on the map with her finger. She stopped where it met the Yellow River – the yellow snake – and followed the river south. She paused at Xi'an. The name looked familiar.

She had come across it last night, when she and Lee were looking for duck-related places in China. That seemed like such a long time ago now, but she remembered why Xi'an was a special place. It was where the first emperor of China was buried, along with an entire army made of terracotta. Nina hadn't known what terracotta was, so she had looked it up in the dictionary. It was a material made of baked earth . . .

That was it! Nina pressed Xi'an on the map. The shed started to shake.

Chapter Nine

"Whoa!" Nina was about to step out of the shed when she realized there was no ground beneath her foot. She quickly retreated.

The shed was balanced on a ledge. Below, an open pit was filled with rows of soldiers, ready to move into battle at any moment.

As Nina took in the still, gloomy silence, she saw that the warriors lined up below her weren't real.

She thought about Lee. She had to get out of the shed, but how? Jumping seemed impossible. The drop was more than two metres, and she would have to avoid crashing into the terracotta statues. That would be very painful indeed. She thought about the students who had split a plank of wood with just one kick, and how she had just solved the fourth line of the riddle. Those things too had seemed impossible.

Nina bent her knees and focused on landing in a little gap between the statues. She felt a hot ball of qi energy gathering up inside her. Her toes began to tingle, and she leaped. She landed on the ground on her hands and knees, unhurt. She had done it!

She stood up, brushed herself off, and walked among the statues.

She was surprised by how real they looked. Each warrior had a unique face, uniform and weapon. As she passed them, she felt as if their eyes were following her.

She quickened her pace. She was sure that, any moment now, one of them would come to life and tap her on the shoulder. She made her way deeper and deeper into the pit. *What if I never find my way out again?* she thought.

Then she heard something – voices! She crept towards the sound, and hid behind a statue when she got close enough.

In the middle of a clearing, two chairs stood side by side. A woman with long black hair and gleaming eyes was bound to one chair with lots of rope. Two big guards stood on either side of her. Next to her, a small bespectacled man sat with the air of someone watching television at home; his hands were tied loosely behind him. Nina guessed that these were Lee's parents, because they were exactly as Master Zhong had described. The

man seemed calm and knowledgeable – yin – and the woman seemed fiery and strong – yang. No wonder they had tied her up so securely. A short man in purple and gold robes paced to and fro before them.

"Stop wasting time! I have done everything in the script: I took you from Beijing, trailed along the Great Wall and the Yellow River—" he said.

"Wasn't necessary," said Lee's dad, with an amused look on his face. "We could have just caught a plane. You shouldn't take these riddles so literally."

"Shut up! When the Great Jin Shi Huang speaks, everyone listens!"

Jin Shi Huang. The name sounded a bit like Qin Shi Huang, who Nina had learned was the first emperor of China.

"Just show me the key like the riddle says – then I can get this whole army up and running and rule China, as is my right!"

"Just because you're a descendant of the first emperor doesn't mean you can have the key!" spat Lee's mum.

All of a sudden, someone came stumbling into the clearing — it was Lee. And he was being pushed along by Master Zhong.

Nina almost gasped, but managed to stop herself just in time. She couldn't risk being found out. From her position behind the statue, she saw that Lee's parents suddenly looked very worried.

"Sorry I'm late, Jin Shi Huang. We missed the first plane because I had to get rid of his companion," said Master Zhong.

Jin Shi Huang turned to Lee's parents with a smile. "Give me the key now, or else your son will be hurt."

"But . . . we can't," said Lee's mum.

Jin Shi Huang nodded and the two guards grabbed Lee.

Nina panicked. She had to do something!

She put her hands in her pockets, not knowing what she hoped to find there, and was jabbed by a bunch of chopsticks.

She remembered something Master Zhong had said: *You can even make a pair of chopsticks fly through the air like daggers!*

Nina leaned round the side of the statue, and quickly threw a chopstick at one of the guards. It bounced off his thigh without him even noticing, but Lee's mother saw and glanced in Nina's direction. Her eyes widened when she spotted Nina.

"Wait!" said Lee's mum.

Master Zhong smiled. "I knew you'd see the light, Kiki. You always were my favourite pupil, even if we did have our differences. Just think, if China were ruled by an emperor again, kung-fu masters would be revered once more! Nowadays children are only interested in computer games and fast food. Our art form is dying. Give him the key to set this army free, so we can return to the golden era."

While Master Zhong was speaking, Nina concentrated on her qi energy. She had to block everything else out and focus. Once more she felt a hot ball of energy gathering inside her. Her arm and fingers began to tingle. She reached for a chopstick.

A jolt of energy shot out of her hand, and the chopstick went spinning through the air. It struck the guard on the head, and he fell over! Everyone looked round in confusion. Nina kept herself hidden.

Jin Shi Huang started shouting while

Master Zhong tried to revive the fallen man. Lee wriggled to escape from the other guard. Lee's mother tipped her chair sideways and picked up the chopstick that had landed near her. She used it to work the ropes around her wrists loose, as if she were untangling a bowl of noodles. The only person who remained still was Lee's dad, who quietly observed the activity around him.

Nina used the energy buzzing inside her to throw another chopstick at the second guard, but he saw it spinning towards him and ducked. He spotted Nina and rushed towards her, but then suddenly went flying through the air. Nina didn't understand what had happened, until she saw that Lee's father had stuck out his foot and tripped the man up!

Lee's mum was now sparring with Master Zhong. Nina was so mesmerized by their fast, smooth kicks and jabs that she didn't notice what Jin Shi Huang was up to.

"Mum!" cried Lee. Jin Shi Huang had captured him and was pointing a spear made of terracotta at him. As Lee's mum turned to look, Master Zhong picked up a chair and was about to hit her with it. Nina flung a pair of chopsticks at him, one after the other. The solid gold chopsticks that he had given her were powerful enough to put him out of action.

"Give me the key or the boy gets hurt," said Jin Shi Huang, still holding onto Lee.

"It's really not that simple," said Lee's father. "If we could give you the key, we would."

"Enough! I don't have time for excuses!" said Jin Shi Huang, prodding Lee with the spear.

Nina reached into her shoe and pulled out the key to the spice shed. She stepped out from behind her statue and held it out.

"Here it is," she said. "This is the key that will set the army free."

Jin Shi Huang let go of Lee and stepped towards Nina, his greedy eyes fixed on the tiny gold key. Lee's mother moved like lightning – she grabbed Jin Shi Huang from behind, threw him into a chair, and tied him up with the rope.

Everyone breathed a sigh of relief.

"I'd be grateful if you could untie me now," said Lee's father.

Chapter Ten

"I told him that riddles shouldn't be taken so literally," said Lee's dad. "You see, there isn't an actual key that sets the army free — it's a special sort of 'qi' that my wife and I generate because of our yin and yang compatibility!"

"Wow," said Nina. "Master Zhong was right — the riddle does get harder as it goes along. Still, I'm surprised he didn't see that last twist!"

"I'm not," said Lee. "It's a bit like how I wouldn't have figured out that Beijing was the place of duck without your help. We sometimes overlook things we're most familiar with. I dread to think what would have happened if we hadn't met. I wish I were as clever and as brave as you!"

"Yes," said his mum, "you have a very good combination of yin and yang – you are both a fighter and a thinker. That is why you have such amazing qi. Now, let's get you into that shed before the police arrive. Explaining things to them and Lee's aunt is going to be tricky enough without having to mention a travelling spice shed!"

Nina was sad to say goodbye to Lee, but he and his parents said that she could come back to China whenever she wanted. Then Nina climbed onto Lee's mum's shoulders and pulled herself up into the shed. Exhausted, she touched London on the map.

When Nina got back to Aunt Nishi's, it was Saturday morning – again! She slipped back into the house, and went upstairs to where Aunt Nishi was still snoring in bed. She could have made up an excuse for Lee's absence and the missing gold necklace, but she wanted to tell the truth.

"Nina, I am disappointed," said Aunt Nishi. "I thought I could trust you. But I have to admit, your intentions were noble and you seem to have learned your lesson."

After Aunt Nishi made her some French-Welsh Rarebit Toast, Nina went to sleep for a very long time.

On Monday morning, Nina fidgeted on her way to school. She knew that Simon would be waiting. She wished Lee was with her, so that they could face him together.

As soon as she walked into school, a big hand grabbed her and dragged her over to the bins.

"So I see your friend was too scared to come in for a binning today," said Simon as he got ready to pick her up.

Nina tried to remain calm. She planted both feet on the ground, bent her legs, and concentrated her qi energy downwards. Simon attempted to pick her up, but he couldn't. He tried harder and harder, until his face was red and puffy and the other children were laughing at him. Angry and humiliated, he turned and slunk away.

"Yes!" said Nina, and entered the school building feeling as if she could achieve anything if she put her mind to it.

About the author

Madhvi Ramani was born in London, where she studied English and then Creative Writing at university. Like Nina, she enjoys having adventures in different countries. She also likes blueberries, dark chocolate and books. She lives in Berlin with her husband and imaginary cat. You can follow her on Twitter @MadhviRamani

Where would you like Nina to travel next? If you have a suggestion, please send a letter to Madhvi Ramani, c/o Tamarind Books, 61–63 Uxbridge Road, London W5 5SA

Nina's Fantastic Facts about China

- As well as snake meat, restaurants in China also offer delicacies such as turtle soup and grasshoppers.

- Many things were invented in China, including silk, paper, gunpowder and the magnetic compass.

- The Great Wall of China is more than 8,000 kilometres long! However, although many people, like Lee, believe that it can be seen with the naked eye from space, this is a myth.

- In China, as well as Mother's Day and Father's Day, they also celebrate Children's Day!

Nina's Guide to Chopstick Etiquette

As Nina discovers, there are many rules when it comes to using chopsticks. Here are some extra tips she picked up while in China:

- If you hit the side of your bowl or plate with your chopsticks and make a lot of noise, people will think you are asking for money!

- It is rude to point at people with your chopsticks.

- Be careful to lay your chopsticks side by side on the table so that they do not cross each other – which is a symbol of death.

- After you have finished eating, you can put your chopsticks across your bowl. That means you are done.

The Chinese Zodiac

Are you a monkey or a rabbit? Find the year you were born in below and discover what animal you are and what it says about your personality, according to Chinese tradition. Do the same for your friends and family!

Rat: You are smart and like parties and making money!
Year: 1936, 1948, 1960, 1972, 1984, 1996, 2008

Ox: You are dependable and honest. You like to get things right first time round.
Year: 1937, 1949, 1961, 1973, 1985, 1997, 2009

Tiger: You are courageous and emotional, and have good leadership skills.
Year: 1938, 1950, 1962, 1974, 1986, 1998, 2010

Rabbit: You are popular, with a large circle of family and friends. You hate arguments.

Year: 1939, 1951, 1963, 1975, 1987, 1999, 2011

Dragon: You are strong, helpful and have an outgoing personality. You can get along with all types of people.

Year: 1940, 1952, 1964, 1976, 1988, 2000, 2012

Snake: You are clever and wise, and you like nice things.

Year: 1941, 1953, 1965, 1977, 1989, 2001, 2013

Horse: You are hard-working, popular and love running around outdoors.

Year: 1942, 1954, 1966, 1978, 1990, 2002, 2014

Sheep: You are good at art and creative activities and like to look good.

Year: 1943, 1955, 1967, 1979, 1991, 2003, 2015

Monkey: You are fun, friendly and a little bit of a show off!
Year: 1944, 1956, 1968, 1980, 1992, 2004, 2016

Rooster: You are hard-working and are good at organizing things. You like to tell the truth.
Year: 1945, 1957, 1969, 1981, 1993, 2005, 2017

Dog: You're loyal, funny and a fantastic listener – all of which makes you a great friend!
Year: 1946, 1958, 1970, 1982, 1994, 2006, 2018

Pig: You are smart, caring and helpful, and you love luxurious things.
Year: 1947, 1959, 1971, 1983, 1995, 2007, 2019

Lee's Favourite
Sugar-Filled Buns (Baozi)

Ingredients:

500g flour
100g white sugar
2 teaspoons yeast
1.5 teaspoons
  baking powder
1 cup warm water
2 tablespoons oil
40 teaspoons brown sugar

What to do:

(Make sure you ask a grown-up to help you!)

1. Mix the flour, white sugar, yeast and baking
   powder together in a large bowl, then add the
   water and oil and combine. Knead the dough
   until it is stretchy and shiny.

2. Form the dough into a ball, put it in a bowl

and cover with a tea towel. Place the bowl in a warm place and let the dough rise for about an hour, until it doubles in size.

3. Punch down the dough and roll it into a rectangle. Cut the rectangle into 20 equal pieces and then roll each piece into a ball. Space the balls apart on a baking sheet and cover with a damp towel. Let the dough rest for 15 minutes.

4. Flatten a piece of dough, put two teaspoons of brown sugar in the middle and then wrap the sides over the filling, pinching them together at the top. Repeat, until you have 20 buns.

5. Place the buns onto separate pieces of parchment paper or cupcake liners, on a steamer tray, leaving space for them to expand. Tightly cover, and steam for about 15-20 minutes, until they are cooked through.

6. Eat warm, or freeze and then re-heat using a steamer or microwave.